To my big bad monster

First Edition, July 2019
10 9 8 7 6 5 4 3 2 1
FAC-029191-19137

Printed in Malaysia

This book is set in Strima/Fontspring.
Designed by Jamie Alloy

Library of Congress Cataloging-in-Publication Data
Names: Kang, A. N., author, illustrator.
Title: My big bad monster / by A. N. Kang. | Description: First edition. | Los Angeles ; New York : Disney Hyperion, 2019. | Summary: "A young girl learns to overcome the monster of self-doubt" —Provided by publisher.
Identifiers: LCCN 2018032598 | ISBN 9781484728826 (hardcover) | ISBN 1484728823 (hardcover)
Subjects: | CYAC: Monsters—Fiction. | Self-confidence—Fiction. | Friendship—Fiction.
Classification: LCC PZ7.1.K26 My 2019 | DDC [E]—dc23
LC record available at https://lccn.loc.gov/2018032598

Reinforced binding
Visit www.DisneyBooks.com

MY BIG BAD MONSTER

BY
A. N. KANG

ZZZZZPT

Disney • HYPERION
Los Angeles   New York

The more she listened . . .

... the more the monster grew ...

. . . and grew.

She started sounding like
the monster, too.

But he wouldn't listen.

So now she wouldn't, either.

I CAN'T HEAR YOU~ LA LA LA

She had so much fun making music,
she decided to create her own instruments.

ZZZzzpt

Then she asked a new
friend to join in.

They sounded spectacular!

The girl never heard from the monster again.
But then, she wasn't listening anyway.
She was just too busy having fun
with her friends!